With *pops* and *bangs*, *poofs* and *splaaats*,
she *whooshed* the kids like acrobats.
Gadoosh's buttons filled the air.
Press Here To Start bounced everywhere.

To my daughter Chantell — for the magic in my heart
To my husband Bob — for the laughter in my soul

A special thanks to Brian Cassidy, my former colleague and mentor at CIBC (Canadian Imperial Bank of Commerce), for teaching me that anything is possible. Thanks also to John Thompson and all the staff at Illumination Arts for their excellent editing and support, and to Andrea Hurst for believing in the wisdom of *Gadoosh*.

Pat Skene

To my wife Beth — for her love, patience and advice
To my daughter Corie Lyn — for her smile that melts our hearts

A special thanks to my family for their continuing support and confidence.
Also to Illumination Arts for their passion and commitment to making beautiful books.

Doug Keith

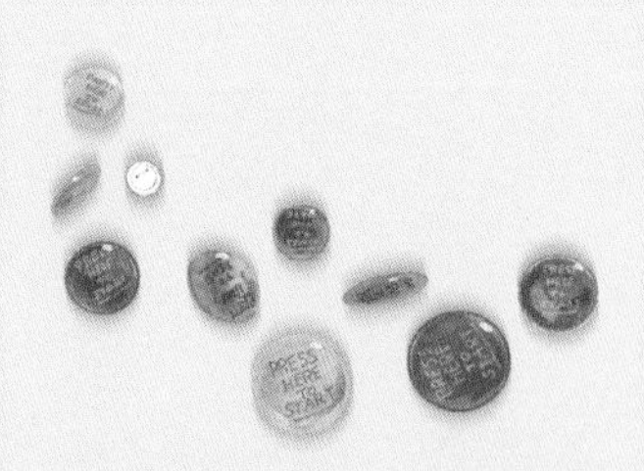

Photo by Cindy Taylor

Pat Skene telling stories at the Ronald McDonald House in Toronto

"**Toronto's Ronald McDonald House** is a 'home away from home' for out of town families whose children are receiving specialized treatment for serious illnesses in Toronto hospitals. Families residing at the House experience feelings of uncertainty and unfamiliarity. Their lives are filled with medical appointments, as well as facts and figures about their child's illness. Pat Skene, our volunteer storyteller, fills the House with fun and laughter every time she reads *The Whoosh of Gadoosh*. This magical story, combined with Pat's powerful storytelling ability, allows parents and children alike to forget for a short time the stresses they are dealing with, and lose themselves in this wonderful fantasy."

Joanne MacKenzie, Executive Director, Toronto's Ronald McDonald House

For further information about Toronto's Ronald McDonald House, please write to them at 26 Gerrard St. E. Toronto, Ontario, Canada M5B1G3 or visit their website at: www.rmhtoronto.org.

A portion of the author's revenues will be donated to Raising The Roof and Ronald McDonald Houses.

THE WHOOSH OF GADOOSH

Written by Pat Skene • Illustrated by Doug Keith

ILLUMINATION Arts
PUBLISHING COMPANY, INC.
BELLEVUE, WASHINGTON

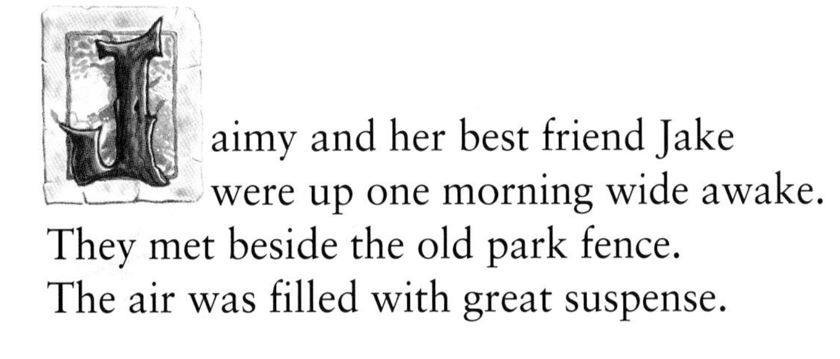

Jaimy and her best friend Jake
were up one morning wide awake.
They met beside the old park fence.
The air was filled with great suspense.

Jake said, "Gadoosh lives on the street.
They say that she's got magic feet.
I hear she sleeps without a bed,
upside down, right on her head.

"She walks each morning through the park
then disappears from view by dark.
She never speaks to anyone,
so no one knows where she is from."

Jaimy pointed, "Over there!
I think I see her purple hair."
From 'round the bend Gadoosh appeared.
Kids ran to meet her as they cheered.

She wore a shawl around her dress.
Her hair looked like a frizzled mess.
Her sparkling eyes began to dance.
The kids adored her at first glance.

She pushed her squeaky cart about,
her shabby shoes flipped inside out.
A cardboard sign, all frayed and bent,
said, “Magic Buttons for One Cent.”

She sold those buttons from her cart,
and each one read, **"Press Here to Start."**
The children loved her *whooshing* game,
and so Gadoosh became her name.

Just then she heard the children call
and parked her cart against the wall.
What happened next was quite profound.
Her inside-out shoes left the ground.

She floated up into the air
and *whooshed* her magic everywhere.
This special magic only came
when children laughed and called her name.

The more they'd laugh, the more she'd *whoosh*.
The more they'd chant, "Gadoosh, Gadoosh!"

PRESS
HERE
TO

With *pops* and *bangs*, *poofs* and *splaaats*,
she *whooshed* the kids like acrobats.
Gadoosh's buttons filled the air.
Press Here To Start bounced everywhere.

Then all at once Jake went, "Aaaah-Chooo!"
The other kids were sneezing too.
They sneezed out pigs in ballet slippers
and leaping frogs with rainbow flippers.

Things were jumping! Things were hot!
All bubbly like a boiling pot.
The scene was quite a ballyhoo.
A topsy-turvy hullabaloo!

Then Jaimy yelled, "It's time for school!
Let's say so long. We know the rule."
So as the children waved goodbye,
Gadoosh let out a wistful sigh.

Then all at once, the magic stopped
and things went quiet, then she dropped.
Her inside-out shoes hit the ground.
She turned to go but made no sound.

So Jake cried out in great dismay,
"We can't just let her walk away."

The kids agreed, "It would be cool
if she could come with us to school."

"Come on, Gadoosh, for Show and Tell.
Let's hurry up. There goes the bell."
Then Jaimy giggled. Jake did too.
They both knew what Miss Pitts would do!

Gadoosh reached in her cart of rags
and pulled some buttons from her bags,
then pinned one over Jaimy's heart.
"Me too," said Jake, "**Press Here To Start!**"

They rushed Gadoosh in through the gate
and ran inside 'cause they were late.
They slid along the polished floor
then opened wide the classroom door.

And when kids saw Gadoosh was there,
they threw their books up in the air!
Dropping pencils, pens and paper,
they raced to join the *whooshing* caper.

The kids sang out, "Gadoosh! Gadoosh!
Come play with us, make things go *whoosh*!"

As laughter filled the corridor,
her inside-out shoes left the floor.
She floated high above their heads,
suspended by her magic threads.

Her buttons bounced with *pings* and *pangs*,
while children flipped like boomerangs.
Cartwheels, handstands, mid-air splits—
and poor Miss Pitts was having fits.

What a frenzy! What a scuffle!
School was in a real kurfuffle!

“Stop all that noise!” Miss Pitts cried out.
She pinched her lips into a pout,
then stamped her foot, which shook her bun.
“This is no time for having fun.”

Then poor Miss Pitts began to sneeze.
She sneezed a dozen chimpanzees.
Miss Pitts was vexed and quite perplexed
and wondered what she should do next.

With monkeys piled up on her head,
“She’s got to go,” the teacher said.
The kids all cried, “Please let her stay.
She needs to be where children play.”

Then Jaimy said, "Let's volunteer!
She has no home; could she live here?
She needs a place that's warm at night,
a place where she will be all right."

Miss Pitts turned red—out came a shriek,
"You want her living *here* all week?
No! No!" she screamed. "We have no space.
You'll have to find another place."

But then before she could resume,
Jake said, "Gadoosh won't need much room.
She doesn't even need a bed,
because she sleeps right on her head."

Miss Pitts gasped and turned chalk-white.
(Perhaps her bun was pinned too tight.)
"Oh, no!" she wailed. "This just won't do.
We'll have to think of something new."

Jaimy thought and thought some more.
She thought so much, her head was sore.
She squished her brains with all her might,
then…FLASH…went her idea-light!

“My gosh, that’s it!” she yelled out loud.
“I’ll solve the problem,” Jaimy vowed.
“I know a place where she can stay,
where they need magic every day.”

She ran outside. “Come follow me.
I know the perfect home, you’ll see!”
They followed Jaimy in a *whoosh*—
Miss Pitts, the children and Gadoosh.

The principal saw them depart,
which made Miss Pitts faint in the cart.
Gadoosh and Jaimy led the gang.
They all marched down the street and sang.

"Hooray, hooray! Gadoosh, Gadoosh!
Come play with us, make things go *whoosh*!"
Gadoosh's buttons filled the air
like magic, bouncing everywhere.

Then Jaimy yelled, "Here's where we stop."
The building had an "H" on top.
Jake recognized the yellow brick.
"Here's where kids come when they get sick."

That's when he squeezed Gadoosh's hand.
She grinned and seemed to understand.
Then Jaimy whispered in her ear,
"Let's go, Gadoosh, they need you here."

H

Just then Miss Pitts awoke and cried,
"We'll stay out here. *You* go inside."
The trio breezed on through the door
and went up to the Children's Floor.

The kids peeked out and squealed, "Gadoosh!
Come play with us, make things go *whoosh*!"
Gadoosh's feet began to rise.
All eyes were filled with great surprise.

She floated up into the air
with flowers sprouting from her hair.
Then magic starlight floated down
and burst like sparklers on the ground.

She *whooshed* and then before their eyes,
whirled cherry cakes and chocolate pies.
The nurses giggled, doctors too.
They didn't know just what to do.

They watched Gadoosh make whirligigs
from stethoscopes and thingamajigs.
Then kids with wheelchairs squealed down halls,
and those with crutches hopped on walls.

One kid was sneezing kangaroos,
while others sneezed out cockatoos!
One wore a sling and plaster cast,
but danced a jig as he whizzed past.

The children cheered, "Gadoosh! Gadoosh!
Please stay with us, make things go *whoosh*!"
If they were sick, you couldn't tell.
Gadoosh had *whooshed* and made them well.

The doctors and the nurses said,
"We sure do like your purple head.
We'd like it if you came to stay.
We need your magic every day."

She answered in a great *kaaaboom*—
a spray of buttons filled the room.
Then rainbows danced above their heads,
and colors splashed down on their beds.

"Gadoosh," said Jaimy, "it's quite clear,
this is your home. They need you here."
"But," Jake cried out, "we'll miss your game.
Our park will never be the same."

“We wish, we wish, Gadoosh, Gadoosh,
that we could *all* make things go *whoosh*.”
That’s when Gadoosh just touched her heart
and pointed to **Press Here To Start.**

When Jake and Jaimy pressed *their* spots,
their buttons burst out polka dots.
As magic sizzled through the air,
it snapped like static in their hair!

Then Jaimy's feet began to rise.
Jake's eyes were bright as fireflies.
"Goodbye," they called out in a *whoosh*.
"We'll always love you, dear Gadoosh."

They floated high above the floor
and flew like starlings out the door.
They laughed and circled Miss Pitts' head.
"We're *whooshing*!" Jake and Jaimy said.

The class all yelled, "Please teach us too!
We'd like to learn to *whoosh* like you."
Then Jaimy said, "It's in your heart.
To *whoosh*, you just **Press Here To Start**."

As one by one, the kids took flight,
Miss Pitts declared with pure delight,
"That looks like fun. Please let me try.
Teach me to *whoosh* so I can fly!"

She giggled, shaking out her bun.
(Miss Pitts had finally come undone.)

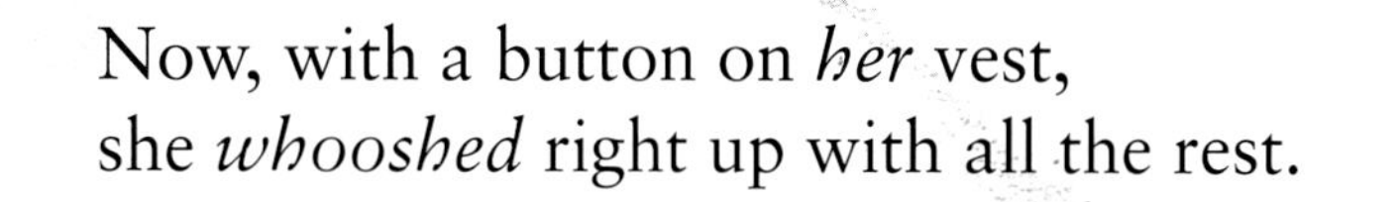

Now, with a button on *her* vest,
she *whooshed* right up with all the rest.

And so they lived forever after,
whooshing magic made of laughter.
The more they'd laugh, the more they'd *whoosh*,
thanks to the magic of Gadoosh.

PRESS
HERE
TO
START

PUBLISHING COMPANY, INC.
P.O. Box 1865, Bellevue, WA 98009
Tel: 425-644-7185 ★ 888-210-8216 (orders only) ★ Fax: 425-644-9274
liteinfo@illumin.com ★ www.illumin.com

Library of Congress Cataloging-in-Publication Data

Skene, Pat, 1945-
The whoosh of Gadoosh / author, Pat Skene ; illustrator, Doug Keith.
p. cm.
Summary: Gadoosh, a purple-haired homeless woman who can magically float aloft on the laughter of children, finds a home in a hospital.
ISBN 0-9701907-0-0
[1. Magic–Fiction. 2. Laughter–Fiction. 3. Hospitals–Fiction. 4. Stories in rhyme.] I. Keith, Doug, ill. II. Title.
PZ8.3.S6195 Wh 2002
[E]–dc21 2001051487

Published in the United States of America
Printed by Star Standard Industries in Singapore
Book Designer: Molly Murrah, Murrah & Company, Kirkland, WA

ILLUMINATION ARTS PUBLISHING COMPANY, INC.
is a member of Publishers in Partnership – replanting our nation's forests.

The Illumination Arts Collection Of Inspiring Children's Books

ALL I SEE IS PART OF ME — by Chara M. Curtis, illustrated by Cynthia Aldrich
In this international bestseller, a child finds the light within his heart and his common link with all of life.

THE BONSAI BEAR — by Bernard Libster, illustrated by Aries Cheung
Issa uses bonsai methods to keep his pet bear small, but the playful cub dreams of following its true nature.

CASSANDRA'S ANGEL — by Gina Otto, illustrated by Trudy Joost
Cassandra feels lonely and misunderstood until a special angel guides her to the truth within.

CORNELIUS AND THE DOG STAR — by Diana Spyropulos, illustrated by Ray Williams
Grouchy old Cornelius Basset-Hound can't enter Dog Heaven until he learns about love, fun and kindness.

THE DOLL LADY — by H. Elizabeth Collins-Varni, illustrated by Judy Kuusisto
The doll lady teaches children to treat dolls kindly and with great love, for they are just like people.

DRAGON — written and illustrated by Jody Bergsma
Born on the same day, a gentle prince and a ferocious, fire-breathing dragon share a prophetic destiny.

DREAMBIRDS — by David Ogden, illustrated by Jody Bergsma
A Native American boy battles his own ego as he searches for the elusive dreambird and its powerful gift.

FUN IS A FEELING — by Chara M. Curtis, illustrated by Cynthia Aldrich
Find your fun! "Fun isn't something or somewhere or who. It's a feeling of joy that lives inside of you."

HOW FAR TO HEAVEN? — by Chara M. Curtis, illustrated by Alfred Currier
Exploring the wonders of nature, Nanna and her granddaughter discover that heaven is all around them.

LITTLE SQUAREHEAD — by Peggy O'Neill, illustrated by Denise Freeman
Rosa overcomes the stigma of her unusual appearance after finding the glowing diamond within her heart.

THE LITTLE WIZARD — written and illustrated by Jody Bergsma
Young Kevin discovers a wizard's cloak while on a perilous mission to save his mother's life.

THE RIGHT TOUCH — by Sandy Kleven, LCSW, illustrated by Jody Bergsma
This award-winning, read-aloud story teaches children how to prevent sexual abuse.

SKY CASTLE — by Sandra Hanken, illustrated by Jody Bergsma
Alive with dolphins, parrots and fairies, this magical tale inspires us to believe in the power of our dreams.

TO SLEEP WITH THE ANGELS — by H. Elizabeth Collins, illustrated by Judy Kuusisto
Comforting her to sleep each night, a young girl's guardian angel fills her dreams with magical adventures.

THE TREE — by Dana Lyons, illustrated by David Danioth
This powerful song of an ancient Douglas fir celebrates the age-old cycle of life in the Pacific Rain Forest.

WHAT IF… — by Regina Williams, illustrated by Doug Keith
Using his fantastic imagination, a little boy delays bedtime for as long as possible. Glow-in-the-dark page included.

WINGS OF CHANGE — by Franklin Hill, Ph.D., illustrated by Aries Cheung
A contented little caterpillar resists his approaching transformation into a butterfly.

ILLUMINATION ARTS PUBLISHING COMPANY, INC.
P.O. Box 1865, Bellevue, WA 98009
Tel: 425-644-7185 ★ 888-210-8216 (orders only) ★ Fax: 425-644-9274
liteinfo@illumin.com ★ www.illumin.com